THE
DOGGONE
MYSTERY

Mary Blount Christian   *Pictures by Irene Trivas*

ALBERT WHITMAN & COMPANY, CHICAGO

Library of Congress Cataloging in Publication Data

Christian, Mary Blount
  The doggone mystery.

  (A First read-alone mystery)
  SUMMARY: Three children and an uncoordinated dog
track down the mastermind behind a rash of household
robberies.
  [1. Mystery and detective stories] I. Trivas,
Irene. II. Title.
PZ7.C4528Do   [E]   80-10448
ISBN 0-8075-1656-2

To Elaine Goley, whose
friendship and encouragement I value

Clara and Jason Brown and their
parents were back from vacation.
Before they went home, they stopped
at Animal Acres. They had to pick up
their dog, Ruffles.

Mr. Bedford, the kennel owner, looked
in his card file. "Your dog has been
here five days," he said. "That's
fifteen dollars." He sent his new
helper, Botts, to get Ruffles.

"Ga-RUFF!" Ruffles greeted the Browns.
She jumped up and licked Jason and
Clara. All the way home, Ruffles
wagged her tail wildly.

When the Browns pulled up to their house,
they saw that something was wrong. Their
front door was wide open.

They rushed inside. Drawers were open.
Clothes were scattered about. "Oh, no!"
Mrs. Brown gasped. "We've been robbed!"

The TV was missing. Clara's radio
was gone. Even Jason's silver baseball
trophy had been stolen. "And it had
my name on it," he groaned.

"Ga-RUFF!" Ruffles barked. She raced
through the house, sniffing and growling.

"Oh, Ruffles!" Jason scolded. "If there
were any fingerprints, you just sniffed
them away!"

The Browns made a list of missing items.
They took the list to the police station.

"We have had a rash of robberies,"
Officer Jolly told them. "Most of the
people robbed were on vacation,
just like you."

"If Ruffles had been home, she would have
scared off the burglar," Jason bragged.

Officer Jolly patted Ruffles's head.
"You may be right," he told Jason. "Dogs
often scare away burglars."

Ruffles knocked over the wastebasket.
"Grrrrr," she growled. "Ga-RUFF!"

Jason set the basket back. "Silly dog,"
he scolded her.

The next day Jason and Clara told
their friend Steve about the burglary.
"We were robbed while we were on
vacation, too," Steve said. "And we
were gone only three days."

"At least they didn't get your dog,"
Clara said.

"Naw," Steve said. "Snuffy was at the
kennel. But they took my bicycle and
record player, and I want them back."

"I want my trophy back, too," Jason said. He jumped up. "Let's be detectives! Ruffles and Snuffy can be our police dogs."

Clara laughed. "Ruffles couldn't find a thief. She's lucky to find her own food dish!"

"Maybe Ruffles won't be much help, but we still might be able to find the thief," Steve said. "Clara, you and Snuffy and I will be partners. Jason, you and Ruffles can work together."

Jason tugged at Ruffles's leash. "Come on, girl," he said. "We can find out who else has been robbed. We'll show Clara and Steve."

Jason rang the Smiths' doorbell. A dog
barked inside.

"Ga-RUFF! Ga-RUFF!" Ruffles barked back.

Mrs. Smith told Jason she and her husband
had been robbed, too. "Our TV and best
silverware were taken," she told him. "We
forgot to stop the newspaper when we
left town. I guess the burglar saw the
paper in the yard and knew we were gone."

Jason wrote that down.

When he was ready to go, he looked
for Ruffles. She was digging in the Smiths' flowers.

"Silly dog!" Jason scolded. "Why
can't you behave?"

Next, Jason and Ruffles went to the
Cotters' house. Sandy Cotter opened the
door. She was holding her new puppy, Sam.

"Ga-RUFF!" Ruffles barked at Sam.

"Grrrr!" Sam barked back. He jumped from
Sandy's arms and ran into the bushes.

Ruffles sat by the bushes and barked,
"Ga-RUFF! Ga-RUFF!"

Sandy told Jason her family had been robbed,
too. "I guess the burglar saw our mail
and knew we were gone," she said. "We
lost a TV and an electric saw."

Jason wrote that down.

At the end of the block, Jason and
Ruffles met Clara, Steve, and Snuffy.

"The Carsons and Bells were robbed,"
Steve said. "The Carsons didn't
leave any lights on. The robber
probably saw that no one was home."

"Ga-RUFF!" Ruffles barked at the
street lamp.

"But the Bells have a light that comes
on by itself," Clara said. "Mrs. Bell
thinks they were robbed during the day."

"Ga-RUFF!" Ruffles barked at a shadow.

18

"Quiet!" Jason scolded. "We're trying
to think!"

"The Bells even told the police they
would be gone," Clara said. "A patrol
car checked the house every night."

"Ga-RUFF!" Ruffles barked. She wound
her leash around the street lamp.

Jason got her loose.

"There must be something we don't see,"
Steve said. "There must be something
everybody has in common. Some of
the people stopped their mail,
but some didn't."

"Some didn't stop their newspapers,
but some did," Clara said.

"And some had the police patrol,"
Jason said.

"Ga-RUFF!" Ruffles said. She wound
her leash around Jason's leg.

"That dog!" Clara grumbled. "If you
don't behave, Ruffles, we'll put you
back in the kennel."

Jason clapped his hands. "The kennel!
Steve, were there dogs at the places
you visited?"

"Naw," Steve said. "The Carsons
and Bells had cats."

Jason shook his head. "I thought maybe the
kennel was the clue. I thought maybe all
the people who were robbed had left
their dogs at the kennel."

21

Steve was excited. "But most kennels
take cats, too!" he said.

Clara gasped. "Animal Acres! Mr. Bedford?
It can't be."

"We've known him forever," Steve told Jason.

"But who knows that guy named Botts?"
Jason asked. "He just started work
at the kennel this summer."

"But how could he know where everybody
lives and how long they'd be away?"
Clara asked.

"Remember the card we filled out?" Jason
said. "We had to give our address and
tell when we were coming back."

"That's it!" Clara said.

The children ran to tell Mr. and Mrs.
Brown what they thought had happened.
Mrs. Brown called the police, and
Officer Jolly came to the house.

"I need your help to catch the thief,"
Officer Jolly said.

The Browns, Steve, and Officer Jolly
made their plans.

On Friday the Browns took Ruffles
to Animal Acres.

"I sure hate to leave our new TV,"
Jason said loudly, so Botts would hear.

"We'll only be gone one night,"
Mr. Brown said.

The Browns waited outside until they saw Botts leave. Then they went back and picked up Ruffles. The five of them drove with Officer Jolly to Steve's house.

"I'm glad Ruffles didn't have to stay
at the kennel tonight, after all," Jason said.

"It's only right that she be here when
we catch the thief." Officer Jolly
winked at Jason.

From a window at Steve's, the Browns
watched their house. After a while,
a truck pulled into the driveway.

"It's Botts," Jason whispered.

Botts broke open the Browns' back door
and slipped inside. Pretty soon he came
out. He was carrying the new TV.

He set the TV in the back of his truck.

"Now!" Officer Jolly said, dashing from
Steve's house. Ruffles followed close
at his heels.

"Hold it, Botts," Officer Jolly called.
"You are under arrest."

"Ga-RUFF! Ga-RUFF!" Ruffles barked.
She tugged on Botts's pants leg
so hard it tore.

"You got him, Ruffles!" Jason yelled.

The next morning the Browns and
Ruffles went to the police station.

"Guess what I found?" Officer Jolly said.
He handed Jason the baseball trophy.
"You kids are good detectives."

Jason laughed. "If Ruffles weren't such
a pest, I wouldn't have thought of the
kennel and Botts."

"In that case," Officer Jolly said,
"Ruffles will be our honorary police dog."

But Ruffles wasn't listening. She had
knocked over the wastebasket.

"Ga-RUFF!" she growled. "Ga-RUFF!"